THE HAUNTING OF BLACK HOLLOW

Zarua D. Maning

CONTENTS

To all the brave souls who venture into the unknown, seeking truth in the shadows.

This book is dedicated to those who confront their fears with unwavering courage, who find light in the darkest places, and who believe in the power of love and determination.

To the spirits who seek peace and to the living who help them find it.

May you find solace in these pages, and may your journey be guided by the light of understanding and compassion.

For the readers who carry the weight of their own haunted histories, this is for you.

With gratitude and hope,

Zarua D. Maning

1

THE INVITATION

Alex adjusted his camera as he scanned the town square of Pinebrook. The quaint, seemingly idyllic town had an unsettling silence. He checked his watch. The rest of the team would arrive soon.

Alex Marlowe, a seasoned paranormal investigator with rugged features and a determined gaze, had always been drawn to the unexplained. His fascination began after a childhood encounter with a spirit in his grandparents' attic. Since then, he'd made it his mission to uncover the truths hidden in the shadows.

The roar of an engine pulled Alex from his thoughts. A dusty SUV pulled up, and Lisa Collins stepped out. With auburn hair tied in a loose ponytail and a leather satchel slung over her shoulder, she looked every bit the dedicated historian. Lisa had joined the team to uncover stories lost to time, driven by the mysterious death of her brother who had vanished while investigating an old asylum.

Mark Bennett, the tech expert, emerged from the passenger side. His wiry frame was hidden beneath a hoodie, and his eyes sparkled with curiosity behind thick glasses. Mark's obsession with technology and the paranormal stemmed from a near-death experience during a lightning storm, which had left him with an unshakable belief in the otherworldly.

Finally, Sarah Reed appeared, stepping out of the backseat. With dark hair cascading around her shoulders and a serene presence, she was the team's medium. Sarah's ability to connect with spirits had both blessed and cursed her, often haunting her dreams—a gift she inherited from her grandmother.

The team exchanged greetings and prepared for their journey to Black Hollow. As they drove through winding roads, the air grew colder, and the trees seemed to close in around them. An elderly local named Henry had given them dire warnings about the mansion, but Alex had brushed them off. After all, they had faced haunted locations before.

They finally arrived at Black Hollow just as the sun dipped below the horizon. The mansion loomed ahead, its gothic architecture a silhouette against the darkening sky. Ivy climbed the stone walls, and shattered windows hinted at the decay within. The air was thick with the scent of damp earth and rot.

As they stepped out of the car, an oppressive silence enveloped them. Alex felt a shiver run down his spine but shook it off. They were here for a reason, and fear wasn't going to stop them.

"Ready?" Alex asked, his voice steady.

The others nodded, though their expressions showed a mix of determination and unease. They approached the mansion's grand entrance, its heavy wooden doors creaking open as if welcoming them to their doom.

2

ENTERING THE MANSION

The interior of Black Hollow was a stark contrast to its once-glorious exterior. The grand foyer was dimly lit by the last rays of the setting sun filtering through cracked stained-glass windows. Dust motes floated in the air, disturbed by their presence.

Lisa ran her fingers over the banister of the grand staircase, feeling the grime and splinters. "This place must have been magnificent once," she murmured, her voice echoing in the cavernous space.

Mark set up his equipment, his movements precise and methodical. "We're getting some strong EMF readings already," he said, adjusting his glasses. "This place is definitely active."

Sarah stood still; her eyes closed as she tried to tune into the mansion's energy. A cold breeze brushed past her, and she shivered, feeling the presence of something unseen.

"Let's start with the main floor," Alex suggested, leading the way. Their footsteps echoed on the marble tiles, amplifying the eerie silence.

They entered a large parlor, its furniture covered in white sheets like ghostly sentinels. A grand piano stood in one corner; its keys yellowed with age. The smell of mildew and decay was stronger here, mixing with the scent of old wood and dust.

Lisa began photographing the room, her camera's

flash briefly illuminating the dark corners. "There's so much history here," she said, her voice tinged with awe. "Imagine the stories these walls could tell."

Mark's devices started beeping, indicating a spike in paranormal activity. "Something's here," he said, his voice low. "Be on your guard."

Sarah felt a chill run through her as she sensed a presence watching them. She could almost hear whispers just out of reach, like the remnants of a long-forgotten conversation.

As they moved deeper into the mansion, the oppressive atmosphere seemed to grow heavier. The air was thick with an indefinable tension, and every creak and groan of the old house set their nerves on edge.

They reached a room that appeared to be a library. Shelves lined the walls, filled with dusty, forgotten tomes. The smell of old books and decaying leather filled the air, a tangible reminder of the mansion's long history.

Lisa's eyes lit up as she scanned the titles. "There's so much to learn here," she said, reaching for a particularly old volume.

But as her fingers touched the book, a cold hand seemed to grip her wrist. She gasped, yanking her hand back and looking around wildly. The others turned to her; concern etched on their faces.

"What happened?" Alex asked, stepping closer.

Lisa shook her head, trying to shake off the lingering cold. "I... I don't know. It felt like someone grabbed me."

Mark checked his equipment, noting another spike in activity. "We're not alone," he said, his voice grim. "Stay close, everyone."

They continued exploring, each step taking them deeper into the mansion's mysteries. The oppressive atmosphere and the sense of being watched never left them, making every moment feel like a prelude to something terrible.

3

THE FIRST ENCOUNTER

As the team ventured further into the mansion, the air grew colder, and the oppressive silence became almost deafening. They entered a large dining hall, its once-grand table now covered in dust and cobwebs. The scent of decay and stale air was overpowering.

Sarah paused, her eyes narrowing as she sensed a presence nearby. "There's something here," she whispered, her voice barely audible.

The room seemed to grow darker as an apparition materialized at the head of the table. It was a ghostly figure of a woman dressed in a tattered gown from a bygone era. Her eyes were hollow, and her face was twisted in an expression of sorrow and rage.

The team froze, their breath caught in their throats. The ghostly woman raised a bony hand, pointing directly at them. "Leave this place," she hissed, her voice echoing through the room like a chilling breeze.

Alex stepped forward, trying to project calm authority. "We mean no harm. We're here to uncover the truth about Black Hollow."

The apparition's eyes seemed to bore into him, filled with a hatred that sent shivers down his spine. "You will find only death here," she warned before dissolving into thin air.

The team stood in stunned silence, the weight of the encounter settling heavily on them. Alex took a deep breath, trying to steady his nerves. "We need to keep moving," he said, though his voice betrayed his own fear.

They continued their exploration, each step feeling like a journey into the unknown. The mansion seemed to pulse with a malevolent energy, and the sense of being watched never left them.

They entered a smaller room, perhaps once a sitting room. The furniture was covered in white sheets, and the smell of mold was overpowering. Sarah walked to the center of the room, her eyes closed as she tried to connect with the spirits.

"I can feel their pain," she whispered, her voice trembling. "So much suffering, so much anger."

Mark's equipment started to beep frantically, indicating another surge in paranormal activity. "We're getting strong readings," he said, his voice tight with tension.

Suddenly, the room grew colder, and the sound of ghostly whispers filled the air. The sheets covering the furniture began to move as if invisible hands were tugging at them. The team huddled together, their fear palpable.

A chair tipped over, crashing to the floor with a loud bang. The whispers grew louder, more insistent, and the temperature continued to drop. Alex tried to remain calm, but the fear gnawed at him.

"We need to stay focused," he said, though his voice wavered. "We're here to uncover the truth, and we can't let fear stop us."

But as the night wore on, it became increasingly clear that the mansion had no intention of letting them leave. The spirits were restless, their anger and pain manifesting in ways that left the team shaken to their core.

4

HISTORY UNVEILED

Lisa was determined to uncover the secrets of Black Hollow. The library held countless volumes, each one a potential key to the mansion's dark past. She ran her fingers over the spines of the books, feeling the rough texture of the aged leather.

"Look at this," she said, pulling out a heavy tome. The cover was embossed with intricate designs, and the pages were yellowed with age. "This might be what we're looking for."

As she opened the book, the musty smell of old paper filled the air. The handwriting was delicate and precise, detailing the history of the Blackwood family. Lisa read aloud, her voice echoing in the silent room.

"The Blackwood family was once one of the most influential families in the region. Their wealth and power were unmatched, but their legacy is shrouded in mystery and tragedy."

She turned the pages, revealing accounts of lavish parties, business dealings, and eventually, the slow descent into darkness. "It seems the family's fortunes took a turn for the worse in the late 1800s. Rumors of dark rituals and mysterious deaths began to circulate."

The team's attention was riveted on Lisa as she continued to read. The stories of betrayal, murder, and dark rituals painted a chilling picture of the mansion's past. The Blackwood family had dabbled in the occult, seeking power and immortality, but their actions had dire consequences.

"Listen to this," Lisa said, her voice trembling. "In 1893, a series of ritualistic sacrifices were performed in the mansion. It was believed that these rituals would grant the family eternal life, but instead, it brought a curse upon them."

The temperature in the room seemed to drop further as she spoke, and the team felt the weight of the mansion's dark history pressing down on them.

Sarah shivered, her connection to the spirits growing stronger. "I can feel their pain," she said softly. "The spirits of those sacrificed are trapped here, their souls unable to find peace."

Mark's equipment beeped in agreement, the readings off the charts. "The energy in this place is unlike anything I've ever seen," he said, his voice tinged with awe and fear.

Alex nodded, his determination hardening. "We need to uncover the truth about what happened here and put these spirits to rest."

But as they delved deeper into the mansion's history, they couldn't shake the feeling that something was watching them—something that did not want its secrets revealed.

5

UNSEEN FORCES

As they moved to the next room, the air grew colder, and the sense of unease intensified. The walls seemed to close in around them, and the shadows grew longer and darker. Mark set up his equipment, the blinking lights and beeping sounds providing a semblance of normalcy in the oppressive atmosphere.

The room they entered appeared to be a study, with a large wooden desk and shelves lined with more books. The smell of old paper and dust was overpowering, and the temperature continued to drop.

"There's definitely something here," Mark said, his voice low. "The readings are off the charts."

Suddenly, the door slammed shut behind them, causing everyone to jump. The oppressive silence was shattered by the sound of footsteps echoing through the room, though no one was there. The air grew even colder, and the team huddled together, their breath visible in the frigid air.

"Stay close," Alex said, his voice steady despite the fear gnawing at him. "We need to stick together."

The sound of whispering filled the room, unintelligible voices overlapping and growing louder. The temperature dropped further, and the sense of dread became almost unbearable. The team could feel an unseen presence watching them, its gaze heavy and malevolent.

Sarah closed her eyes, trying to connect with the spirits. "They're angry," she said, her voice trembling. "They're trapped here, and they blame us for disturbing them."

The whispers grew louder, more insistent, and objects in the room began to move on their own. Books flew off the shelves, papers scattered, and the desk drawer opened and slammed shut repeatedly. The team could feel the presence growing stronger, its anger palpable.

Lisa clutched her camera, capturing the paranormal activity. "We need to find out what they want," she said, her voice barely audible over the cacophony.

Sarah focused, her connection to the spirits growing stronger. "They want us to leave," she said, her voice strained. "But we can't. We need to help them find peace."

The temperature dropped to freezing, and the

whispering voices turned into screams. The team felt a crushing weight pressing down on them as if the very air was trying to suffocate them. The unseen forces were growing more violent, their anger manifesting in physical attacks.

"Everyone stay calm," Alex said, though his own fear was evident. "We need to find a way to communicate with them."

Mark's equipment beeped frantically, indicating a surge in paranormal activity. "We're getting some strong readings," he said, his voice tight with tension.

The oppressive atmosphere and the violent paranormal activity left the team shaken and scared. They knew they were in over their heads, but they couldn't turn back now. They had to uncover the truth about Black Hollow and put the spirits to rest, no matter the cost

6

THE HIDDEN ROOM

The team continued their exploration, the oppressive atmosphere growing heavier with each step. They reached a large hallway lined with portraits of the Blackwood family. The faces in the paintings seemed to watch them, their eyes following their every move.

Sarah paused; her gaze fixed on a portrait of a woman with dark, piercing eyes. "This is the woman I saw earlier," she said, her voice trembling. "She's one of the spirits trapped here."

Lisa examined the portrait, noting the name engraved on the plaque beneath it. "Lady Evelyn Blackwood," she read aloud. "She was the matriarch of the family during their darkest days."

Mark's equipment beeped, indicating a surge in paranormal activity. "There's something behind this wall," he said, his voice filled with curiosity.

Alex examined the wall, his fingers tracing the edges of the portrait. "There's a hidden room here," he said, feeling a slight draft. "Help me move this."

With Mark's help, Alex pushed the portrait aside, revealing a narrow passageway. The air inside was musty and cold, and the smell of mold and decay was overpowering. The team hesitated, the oppressive atmosphere making it hard to breathe.

"We have to see what's in there," Alex said, his voice steady despite the fear gnawing at him.

They squeezed through the narrow passageway, entering a small, dark room. The walls were lined with shelves filled with jars and bottles; each one labeled with strange symbols. The smell of old herbs and dried blood filled the air, and the temperature dropped even further.

"This must have been a ritual room," Lisa said, her voice barely audible. "Look at all these artifacts."

Sarah shivered, her connection to the spirits growing stronger. "I can feel their pain," she said, her voice trembling. "This is where the sacrifices took place."

Mark's equipment beeped frantically, indicating a surge in paranormal activity. "We're getting some strong readings," he said, his voice tight with tension.

Alex examined the shelves, his fingers brushing against the dusty jars. "These symbols are ancient," he said, his voice filled with awe. "They were trying to summon something."

Suddenly, the temperature dropped to freezing, and the room was plunged into darkness. The oppressive silence was shattered by the sound of ghostly whispers and the smell of burning herbs. The team felt a crushing weight pressing down on them as if the very air was trying to suffocate them.

The whispering voices grew louder, more insistent, and the jars and bottles began to rattle on the shelves. The team huddled together; their fear palpable. They knew they were in over their heads, but they couldn't turn back now. They had to uncover the truth about Black Hollow and put the spirits to rest, no matter the cost.

7

SARAH'S VISION

The oppressive darkness seemed to close in around them, and Sarah felt an overwhelming sense of dread. She closed her eyes, trying to connect with the spirits. The air grew colder, and the smell of burning herbs filled her nostrils.

Suddenly, she was transported to another time. The small, dark room was now illuminated by the flickering light of candles. She saw Lady Evelyn Blackwood standing in the center of the room, surrounded by hooded figures. The air was thick with the scent of burning herbs and the metallic tang of blood.

Lady Evelyn's eyes were filled with a malevolent intensity as she chanted in an ancient language. The hooded figures echoed her words, their voices blending into a haunting melody. In the center of the room lay a young woman, bound and gagged, her eyes wide with terror.

Sarah felt the young woman's fear and pain as if it were her own. The ritual reached its climax, and Lady Evelyn raised a dagger, its blade glinting in the candlelight. The young woman's screams were muffled by the gag, and Sarah felt a surge of horror as the dagger plunged into her heart.

The room was filled with the scent of fresh blood and the sound of the woman's dying breaths. The hooded figures chanted louder; their voices filled with a manic fervor. The air crackled with dark energy, and Sarah felt a crushing weight pressing down on her chest.

She gasped, her eyes flying open as she was yanked back to the present. The small, dark room was still filled with the oppressive darkness, and the ghostly whispers had grown louder. The team was watching her with concern, their faces pale with fear.

"I saw it," Sarah said, her voice trembling. "I saw the ritual. Lady Evelyn and the others... they sacrificed a young woman. They believed it would grant them eternal life."

The team listened in stunned silence as Sarah recounted her vision. The horror of the ritual and the pain of the young woman were palpable in her words. They could feel the weight of the mansion's dark history pressing down on them.

"We need to find a way to put these spirits to rest," Alex said, his voice steady despite the fear gnawing at him. "We can't let their suffering continue."

Mark's equipment beeped frantically, indicating a

surge in paranormal activity. "The energy in this place is off the charts," he said, his voice tight with tension. "We need to be careful."

The oppressive atmosphere and the violent paranormal activity left the team shaken and scared. They knew they were in over their heads, but they couldn't turn back now. They had to uncover the truth about Black Hollow and put the spirits to rest, no matter the cost.

8

THE BASEMENT

The team gathered their courage and made their way to the basement. The narrow staircase was steep and uneven, and the walls were damp and cold. The smell of mold and decay was overpowering, and the air was thick with a sense of foreboding.

As they descended into the darkness, the temperature dropped further, and the oppressive atmosphere grew heavier. Mark's equipment beeped frantically, indicating a surge in paranormal activity. The team could feel the presence of something malevolent watching them.

They reached the bottom of the stairs, entering a large, dimly lit basement. The walls were lined with old, rusty pipes, and the floor was covered in dirt and debris. The smell of mold and decay was stronger here, mixing with the metallic scent of old blood.

"This place is a nightmare," Lisa said, her voice barely audible. "It's like a tomb."

Sarah shivered, her connection to the spirits growing stronger. "I can feel their pain," she said, her voice trembling. "The spirits of those sacrificed are trapped here, their souls unable to find peace."

The team moved cautiously through the basement, their flashlights casting eerie shadows on the walls. They could hear the sound of ghostly whispers growing louder and more insistent. The temperature continued to drop, and the sense of dread became almost unbearable.

Suddenly, the air grew colder, and the smell of decay intensified. A ghostly figure materialized before them, its eyes filled with sorrow and rage. It was the spirit of a young woman, her face twisted in pain and despair.

The team froze, their breath caught in their throats. The ghostly woman raised a bony hand, pointing directly at them. "Help us," she whispered, her voice filled with anguish. "Release us from this torment."

Sarah stepped forward, her heart pounding in her chest. "We will," she said, her voice steady despite the fear gnawing at her. "We will find a way to free you."

The spirit's eyes seemed to bore into Sarah's soul, filled with a mixture of hope and despair. "Hurry," she whispered before dissolving into thin air.

The team stood in stunned silence, the weight of the encounter settling heavily on them. They knew they had to find a way to put the spirits to rest, but the task seemed insurmountable.

"We need to keep moving," Alex said, his voice steady despite the fear gnawing at him. "We can't let fear stop us."

The team continued their exploration, each step taking them deeper into the mansion's mysteries. The oppressive atmosphere and the sense of being watched never left them, making every moment feel like a prelude to something terrible.

9

MARK'S DISAPPEARANCE

The oppressive atmosphere and the violent paranormal activity left the team shaken and scared. They knew they were in over their heads, but they couldn't turn back now. They had to uncover the truth about Black Hollow and put the spirits to rest, no matter the cost.

They continued exploring the basement, their flashlights casting eerie shadows on the walls. The air grew colder, and the smell of mold and decay was overpowering. The sound of ghostly whispers filled the air, growing louder and more insistent.

Suddenly, Mark's equipment beeped frantically, indicating a surge in paranormal activity. "Something's happening," he said, his voice tight with tension.

Before they could react, the lights on Mark's equipment went out, plunging them into darkness. The oppressive silence was shattered by the sound of footsteps echoing through the basement, though no one was there.

"Stay close," Alex said, his voice steady despite the fear gnawing at him.

The team huddled together, their flashlights flickering as they tried to find their way. The air grew colder, and the ghostly whispers turned into screams. The sense of dread became almost unbearable.

Suddenly, Mark was yanked away from the group,

his scream echoing through the basement. The team turned their flashlights, searching the darkness, but Mark was gone.

"Mark!" Alex shouted; his voice filled with panic. "Where are you?"

The oppressive silence returned, and the team could feel the presence of something malevolent watching them. They knew they had to find Mark, but the darkness seemed to close in around them, making it hard to breathe.

"Stay calm," Alex said, though his own fear was evident. "We need to find him."

They searched the basement, calling out Mark's name, but there was no response. The oppressive atmosphere and the sense of being watched never left them, making every moment feel like a prelude to something terrible.

As they moved deeper into the basement, they discovered a secret passage. The walls were lined with old, rusty pipes, and the floor was covered in dirt and debris. The smell of mold and decay was overpowering.

"This must be where Mark went," Lisa said, her voice trembling.

The team squeezed through the narrow passage, their flashlights casting eerie shadows on the walls. The air grew colder, and the sense of dread became almost unbearable.

They reached a small, dimly lit room, and their flashlights revealed Mark lying on the floor, unconscious. The air was thick with the smell of decay and old blood, and the temperature had dropped to freezing.

"Mark!" Alex shouted, rushing to his side.

Mark's eyes fluttered open, and he groaned, his face pale with fear. "I... I saw something," he said, his voice barely audible. "It was trying to take me."

The team helped Mark to his feet, their fear and

determination mingling. They knew they had to uncover the truth about Black Hollow and put the spirits to rest, no matter the cost.

10

THE DIARY

The oppressive atmosphere and the violent paranormal activity left the team shaken and scared. They knew they were in over their heads, but they couldn't turn back now. They had to uncover the truth about Black Hollow and put the spirits to rest, no matter the cost.

They returned to the main floor, hoping to find some answers. Lisa was determined to uncover the secrets of Black Hollow, and the library held countless volumes, each one a potential key to the mansion's dark past.

She ran her fingers over the spines of the books, feeling the rough texture of the aged leather. "Look at this," she said, pulling out a heavy tome. The cover was embossed with intricate designs, and the pages were yellowed with age. "This might be what we're looking for."

As she opened the book, the musty smell of old paper filled the air. The handwriting was delicate and precise, detailing the history of the Blackwood family. Lisa read aloud, her voice echoing in the silent room.

"The Blackwood family was once one of the most influential families in the region. Their wealth and power were unmatched, but their legacy is shrouded in mystery and tragedy."

She turned the pages, revealing accounts of lavish parties, business dealings, and eventually, the slow descent into darkness. "It seems the family's fortunes took a turn for the worse in the late 1800s. Rumors of dark rituals and mysterious deaths began to circulate."

The team's attention was riveted on Lisa as she continued to read. The stories of betrayal, murder, and dark rituals painted a chilling picture of the mansion's past. The Blackwood family had dabbled in the occult, seeking power and immortality, but their actions had dire consequences.

"Listen to this," Lisa said, her voice trembling. "In 1893, a series of ritualistic sacrifices were performed in the mansion. It was believed that these rituals would grant the family eternal life, but instead, it brought a curse upon them."

The temperature in the room seemed to drop further as she spoke, and the team felt the weight of the mansion's dark history pressing down on them.

Sarah shivered, her connection to the spirits growing stronger. "I can feel their pain," she said softly. "The spirits of those sacrificed are trapped here, their souls unable to find peace."

Mark's equipment beeped in agreement, the readings off the charts. "The energy in this place is unlike anything I've ever seen," he said, his voice tinged with awe and fear.

Alex nodded, his determination hardening. "We need to uncover the truth about what happened here and put these spirits to rest."

But as they delved deeper into the mansion's history, they couldn't shake the feeling that something was watching them—something that did not want its secrets revealed.

11

TRAPPED

The team's resolve hardened as they gathered their thoughts in the library. Alex, Mark, Lisa, and Sarah knew they had to uncover more about the curse that had doomed the Blackwood family and trapped the spirits within Black Hollow.

As they prepared to leave the library, a loud crash echoed from the hallway. They rushed out to find the mansion's heavy doors and windows sealed shut, as if the house itself had decided to imprison them. The scent of old wood and decaying plaster filled the air, mingling with the cold draft that seemed to come from nowhere.

"We're trapped," Lisa said, her voice barely above a whisper. Panic laced her words.

"We need to stay calm," Alex responded, though his own heart raced. "There's got to be another way out."

Mark's equipment beeped, indicating another surge in paranormal activity. "The energy readings are spiking again," he said, his voice tight with tension.

Sarah closed her eyes, trying to connect with the spirits. "They're angry," she said, her voice trembling. "They're trying to keep us here."

The team moved cautiously through the mansion, searching for another exit. Each step they took echoed ominously in the darkened halls. The oppressive atmosphere and the sense of being watched never left them, making every moment feel like a prelude to something terrible.

They reached a grand ballroom, its once-glorious decor now faded and covered in dust. The chandeliers hung precariously from the ceiling, and the smell of mold and decay was overpowering. The air was thick with tension, and the temperature continued to drop.

As they explored the room, the sound of ghostly music filled the air. The team turned their flashlights, revealing ghostly figures dancing in the ballroom. The spirits moved with an eerie grace, their faces twisted in sorrow and despair.

Sarah stepped forward, trying to communicate with the spirits. "Why are you here?" she asked, her voice steady despite the fear gnawing at her.

One of the spirits, a woman in a tattered ball gown, turned to Sarah. "We are trapped, just like you," she said, her voice a haunting whisper. "We cannot leave until the curse is broken."

The team listened in stunned silence as the ghostly woman recounted the events that had led to their entrapment. The Blackwood family's dark rituals had unleashed a malevolent force that now fed on the fear and souls of those who entered the mansion.

"We must find a way to break the curse," Alex said, his determination hardening. "We can't let these spirits suffer any longer."

But as the ghostly figures continued to dance, the team couldn't shake the feeling that the mansion itself was alive, its malevolent presence growing stronger with each passing moment. The oppressive atmosphere and the sense of being watched left them shaken and scared, but they knew they had to uncover the truth about Black Hollow and put the spirits to rest, no matter the cost.

12

THE BLACKWOOD CURSE

As they left the ballroom, the team made their way to a study filled with old documents and artifacts. Lisa was determined to find more information about the Blackwood curse. The smell of old paper and ink filled the air as she rummaged through the drawers and shelves.

"These documents might hold the key to understanding the curse," Lisa said, her voice filled with determination. She carefully examined each piece of paper, her eyes scanning the delicate handwriting and ancient symbols.

Sarah stood nearby; her eyes closed as she tried to connect with the spirits. The oppressive atmosphere and the sense of being watched never left her, but she knew she had to stay focused. "I can feel their pain," she said softly. "The spirits are desperate for release."

Mark's equipment beeped, indicating another surge in paranormal activity. "The energy in this room is off the charts," he said, his voice tight with tension. "We need to be careful."

As Lisa continued to sift through the documents, she found a diary belonging to Lady Evelyn Blackwood. The cover was worn, and the pages were yellowed with age. The smell of old leather and ink filled the air as she opened the diary and began to read.

"Lady Evelyn was the one who initiated the dark

rituals," Lisa said, her voice trembling. "She believed that by sacrificing innocent lives, she could grant her family eternal life. But the rituals went horribly wrong, and instead of gaining immortality, they unleashed a malevolent force that cursed the mansion and trapped the spirits of those sacrificed."

The team listened in stunned silence as Lisa read aloud the details of the rituals. The horror of the events and the pain of the victims were palpable in her words. They could feel the weight of the mansion's dark history pressing down on them.

"We need to find a way to break the curse," Alex said, his voice steady despite the fear gnawing at him. "We can't let their suffering continue."

But as they delved deeper into the mansion's history, they couldn't shake the feeling that something was watching them—something that did not want its secrets revealed.

13

MARK'S FATE

The oppressive atmosphere and the violent paranormal activity left the team shaken and scared. They knew they were in over their heads, but they couldn't turn back now. They had to uncover the truth about Black Hollow and put the spirits to rest, no matter the cost.

As they continued their exploration, Mark began to show signs of distress. He was pale and sweating, his eyes wide with fear. The team could see the toll the mansion was taking on him.

"Are you okay, Mark?" Alex asked, his voice filled with concern.

Mark shook his head, his voice barely above a whisper. "I feel like something's inside me," he said, his voice trembling. "It's trying to take control."

The team exchanged worried glances. They knew they had to find a way to help Mark, but the malevolent presence in the mansion seemed to grow stronger with each passing moment.

Sarah closed her eyes, trying to connect with the spirits. "They're angry," she said, her voice filled with sorrow. "They're trying to take him."

The team moved cautiously through the mansion, their flashlights casting eerie shadows on the walls. The air grew colder, and the smell of mold and decay was overpowering. The sense of dread became almost unbearable.

Suddenly, Mark let out a blood-curdling scream and collapsed to the floor. The team rushed to his side, their fear and desperation mingling. They could see the struggle in his eyes, the malevolent force trying to take control.

"We need to do something," Lisa said, her voice trembling. "We can't let him be taken."

Alex grabbed Mark's hand, his voice steady despite the fear gnawing at him. "Mark, you have to fight it," he said, his voice filled with determination. "We're here for you."

The team watched in horror as Mark's body convulsed, his eyes rolling back in his head. The oppressive atmosphere and the violent paranormal activity left them shaken and scared. They knew they had to find a way to break the curse and put the spirits to rest, no matter the cost.

Sarah focused her energy, trying to connect with the spirits and push the malevolent force away from Mark. The air grew colder, and the smell of decay intensified. The sense of dread became almost unbearable.

Finally, with a final agonized scream, Mark's body went limp. The oppressive atmosphere seemed to lift slightly, and the team could feel the malevolent presence retreating.

"Mark, are you okay?" Alex asked, his voice filled with concern.

Mark's eyes fluttered open, and he groaned, his face pale with fear. "I... I think it's gone," he said, his voice barely audible. "But we need to hurry. We don't have much time."

The team helped Mark to his feet, their fear and determination mingling. They knew they had to uncover the truth about Black Hollow and put the spirits to rest, no matter the cost.

14

THE MIRROR ROOM

The oppressive atmosphere and the violent paranormal activity left the team shaken and scared, but they knew they had to press on. They were standing in the heart of the mansion, the source of its malevolent power, and they needed to find a way to destroy it.

Lisa's eyes scanned the chamber, her mind racing as she tried to make sense of the dark energy pulsating through the walls. "We need to find the source of this power," she said, her voice filled with determination. "There has to be something here that we can use to break the curse."

As she examined the walls, she noticed a series of ancient symbols etched into the stone. The smell of old blood and decay filled the air, and the temperature continued to drop. The oppressive atmosphere and the sense of being watched never left them, making every moment feel like a prelude to something terrible.

"These symbols," Lisa said, her voice trembling. "They're part of the ritual. If we can find a way to disrupt them, we might be able to weaken the mansion's power."

Sarah closed her eyes, focusing her energy on the symbols. "I can feel their pain," she said, her voice filled with sorrow. "The spirits are trapped within these walls, their souls bound by the dark energy."

Mark's equipment beeped frantically, indicating a surge in paranormal activity. "The readings are off the charts," he said, his voice tight with tension. "We need to be careful."

As Lisa continued to examine the symbols, she discovered a hidden passage behind one of the walls. The air inside was musty and cold, and the smell of decay was overpowering. The team knew they had to enter the passage, no matter how dangerous it seemed.

They squeezed through the narrow opening, their flashlights casting eerie shadows on the walls. The air grew colder, and the sense of dread became almost unbearable. The passage led them to a small chamber, its walls covered in ancient symbols and dark energy.

"This is it," Lisa said, her voice trembling. "This is the source of the mansion's power."

The team could feel the malevolent presence growing stronger, its dark energy pulsating through the walls. They knew they had to act quickly to put an end to the curse and free the spirits trapped within Black Hollow.

"We need to destroy these symbols," Alex said, his voice steady despite the fear gnawing at him. "It's the only way to break the curse."

Sarah focused her energy, trying to connect with the spirits and push the malevolent force away. The air grew colder, and the smell of decay intensified. The sense of dread became almost unbearable.

As they began to destroy the symbols, the walls around them seemed to come alive, twisting and writhing as if in agony. The oppressive atmosphere and the violent paranormal activity left them shaken and scared, but they knew they had to press on.

Finally, with a final agonized scream, the dark energy began to dissipate, and the oppressive atmosphere seemed to lift slightly. The team could feel the malevolent presence retreating.

"We did it," Lisa said, her voice filled with relief. "We weakened the mansion's power."

But the team knew their work was far from over. The oppressive atmosphere and the violent paranormal activity left them shaken and scared, but they knew they had to uncover the truth about Black Hollow and put the spirits to rest, no matter the cost.

15

THE ATTIC

The oppressive atmosphere seemed to lift slightly, but the team knew their ordeal was far from over. They had weakened the mansion's power, but they still needed to find a way to put the spirits to rest and ensure the curse was truly broken.

They made their way to the attic, the highest point in the mansion, hoping to find more clues. The narrow staircase creaked under their weight, and the smell of dust and decay grew stronger with each step. The air was thick with tension, and the temperature continued to drop.

The attic was a labyrinth of old trunks, forgotten belongings, and cobweb-covered rafters. The team moved cautiously through the cluttered space, their flashlights casting eerie shadows on the walls. The oppressive atmosphere and the sense of being watched never left them, making every moment feel like a prelude to something terrible.

"We need to find anything that can help us break the curse," Alex said, his voice steady despite the fear gnawing at him.

Lisa rummaged through an old trunk, the smell of aged leather and dust filling the air. "There has to be something here," she said, her voice filled with determination. "Something that can help us put the spirits to rest."

Mark's equipment beeped, indicating another surge in paranormal activity. "The energy readings are spiking again," he said, his voice tight with tension. "We need to be careful."

Sarah closed her eyes, trying to connect with the spirits. "I can feel their pain," she said softly. "They're still trapped, still suffering."

As they searched the attic, they stumbled upon a hidden compartment in the floor. The air inside was musty and cold, and the smell of decay was overpowering. The team knew they had to open it, no matter how dangerous it seemed.

They pried open the compartment, revealing a cache of dark ritualistic artifacts. The sight of the objects sent a chill down their spines, and the oppressive atmosphere grew heavier.

"These artifacts must have been used in the rituals," Lisa said, her voice trembling. "We need to destroy them."

As they began to gather the artifacts, the air grew colder, and the sound of ghostly whispers filled the attic. The oppressive atmosphere and the sense of being watched never left them, making every moment feel like a prelude to something terrible.

Suddenly, a ghostly figure materialized before them. It was Lady Evelyn Blackwood, her eyes filled with a malevolent intensity. "You cannot stop us," she hissed, her voice echoing through the attic. "The curse will never be broken."

The team froze, their breath caught in their throats. The ghostly figure raised a bony hand, pointing directly at them. "You will all suffer the same fate," she warned before dissolving into thin air.

The oppressive atmosphere and the violent paranormal activity left the team shaken and scared, but they knew they had to press on. They had to destroy the artifacts and put an end to the curse, no matter the cost.

As they gathered the artifacts, the walls of the attic seemed to close in around them, pulsating with dark energy. The oppressive atmosphere and the sense of being watched never left them, making every moment feel like a prelude to something terrible.

"We need to hurry," Alex said, his voice steady despite the fear gnawing at him. "We can't let the spirits stop us."

The team worked quickly, destroying the artifacts and weakening the mansion's power. The oppressive atmosphere seemed to lift slightly, and the team could feel the malevolent presence retreating.

"We did it," Lisa said, her voice filled with relief. "We destroyed the artifacts."

But the team knew their work was far from over. The oppressive atmosphere and the violent paranormal activity left them shaken and scared, but they knew they had to uncover the truth about Black Hollow and put the spirits to rest, no matter the cost.

16

ALEX'S BATTLE

The oppressive atmosphere and the violent paranormal activity left the team shaken and scared, but they knew they had to press on. They had destroyed the artifacts and weakened the mansion's power, but the malevolent presence still lingered.

As they made their way back down from the attic, the walls seemed to pulse with a dark, sinister energy. The air was thick with tension, and the temperature continued to drop. The sense of dread became almost unbearable.

Suddenly, the mansion seemed to shift around them, the walls closing in, and the floor buckling beneath their feet. The oppressive atmosphere and the sense of being watched never left them, making every moment feel like a prelude to something terrible.

"What's happening?" Lisa asked, her voice trembling with fear.

"The mansion is fighting back," Mark said, his voice tight with tension. "It's trying to stop us."

As they moved through the darkened halls, Alex felt a sudden, overwhelming force pressing down on him. The air grew colder, and the smell of decay intensified. The oppressive atmosphere became suffocating.

"Stay close," Alex said, his voice steady despite the fear gnawing at him. "We need to stick together."

But as they continued to move forward, Alex felt the malevolent presence growing stronger, its dark energy pulsating through the walls. He knew he had to confront it, no matter the cost.

"I'll go ahead," Alex said, his voice filled with determination. "I need to face this thing head-on."

The team exchanged worried glances, but they knew Alex was right. They had to put an end to the malevolent presence once and for all.

Alex moved forward, his flashlight casting eerie shadows on the walls. The air grew colder, and the oppressive atmosphere became almost unbearable. The sense of dread gnawed at him, but he pressed on.

He reached a large chamber, its walls covered in dark, pulsating veins. The air was thick with the smell of decay and old blood, and the temperature had dropped to freezing. The oppressive atmosphere and the sense of being watched never left him, making every moment feel like a prelude to something terrible.

"This is it," Alex said, his voice steady despite the fear gnawing at him. "This is the heart of the mansion."

The malevolent presence seemed to grow stronger, its dark energy pulsating through the walls. Alex could feel the weight of the mansion's dark history pressing down on him, but he knew he had to press on.

As he moved forward, the walls seemed to come alive, twisting and writhing as if in agony. The oppressive atmosphere and the violent paranormal activity left him shaken and scared, but he knew he had to press on.

Suddenly, the air grew colder, and the room was plunged into darkness. The oppressive silence was shattered by the sound of ghostly whispers and the smell of burning herbs. Alex felt a crushing weight pressing down on him, as if the very air was trying to suffocate him.

He focused his energy, trying to push the malevolent force away. The air crackled with dark energy, and the oppressive atmosphere became almost unbearable. But Alex pressed on, his determination unwavering.

Finally, with a final agonized scream, the dark energy began to dissipate, and the oppressive atmosphere seemed to lift slightly. Alex could feel the malevolent presence retreating.

"We did it," Alex said, his voice filled with relief. "We weakened the mansion's power."

But Alex knew his work was far from over. The oppressive atmosphere and the violent paranormal activity left him shaken and scared, but he knew he had to uncover the truth about Black Hollow and put the spirits to rest, no matter the cost.

17

THE MANSION'S HEART

The oppressive atmosphere seemed to lift slightly, but the team knew their ordeal was far from over. They had weakened the mansion's power, but the malevolent presence still lingered. They needed to destroy the source of the mansion's dark energy once and for all.

The team gathered their courage and made their

way deeper into the mansion. The walls pulsed with a dark, sinister energy, and the air was thick with tension. The smell of decay and old blood filled their nostrils, making it hard to breathe.

"We need to find the core of this place," Lisa said, her voice steady despite the fear gnawing at her. "That's where we'll find the source of its power."

Mark's equipment beeped frantically, indicating a surge in paranormal activity. "The readings are off the charts," he said, his voice tight with tension. "We're getting close."

As they moved through the darkened halls, the oppressive atmosphere grew heavier. The sense of dread became almost unbearable, and the temperature continued to drop. The team could feel the malevolent presence watching them, its gaze heavy and malevolent.

They reached a large, ornate door, its surface covered in intricate carvings of ancient symbols. The air around it crackled with dark energy, and the oppressive atmosphere became suffocating.

"This is it," Alex said, his voice filled with determination. "This is the heart of the mansion."

The team exchanged worried glances, but they knew they had to press on. They pushed open the heavy door, revealing a large chamber filled with dark, pulsating veins. The air was thick with the smell of decay and old blood, and the temperature had dropped to freezing.

The oppressive atmosphere and the sense of being watched never left them, making every moment feel like a prelude to something terrible. The malevolent presence seemed to grow stronger, its dark energy pulsating through the walls.

"We need to destroy this place," Lisa said, her voice trembling. "It's the only way to break the curse."

The team moved cautiously through the chamber, their flashlights casting eerie shadows on the walls. The air grew colder, and the oppressive atmosphere became almost unbearable.

Suddenly, the room was plunged into darkness, and the oppressive silence was shattered by the sound of ghostly whispers and the smell of burning herbs. The team felt a crushing weight pressing down on them, as if the very air was trying to suffocate them.

The malevolent presence seemed to grow stronger, its dark energy pulsating through the walls. The team could feel the weight of the mansion's dark history pressing down on them, but they knew they had to press on.

"We need to destroy these symbols," Alex said, his voice steady despite the fear gnawing at him. "It's the only way to break the curse."

Sarah focused her energy, trying to connect with the spirits and push the malevolent force away. The air grew colder, and the smell of decay intensified. The sense of dread became almost unbearable.

As they began to destroy the symbols, the walls around them seemed to come alive, twisting and writhing as if in agony. The oppressive atmosphere and the violent paranormal activity left them shaken and scared, but they knew they had to press on.

Finally, with a final agonized scream, the dark energy began to dissipate, and the oppressive atmosphere seemed to lift slightly. The team could feel the malevolent presence retreating.

"We did it," Lisa said, her voice filled with relief. "We weakened the mansion's power."

But the team knew their work was far from over. The oppressive atmosphere and the violent paranormal activity left them shaken and scared, but they knew they had to uncover the truth about Black Hollow and put the spirits to rest, no matter the cost.

18

THE FINAL RITUAL

The oppressive atmosphere seemed to lift slightly, but the team knew their ordeal was far from over. They had weakened the mansion's power, but the malevolent presence still lingered. They needed to perform the final ritual to break the curse and put the spirits to rest once and for all.

The team gathered their courage and prepared for the final ritual. They knew it would be dangerous, but they were determined to put an end to the mansion's dark history and free the trapped spirits.

Lisa gathered the ancient texts and artifacts they had discovered, carefully laying them out in the center of the chamber. The air was thick with tension, and the temperature continued to drop. The oppressive atmosphere and the sense of being watched never left them, making every moment feel like a prelude to something terrible.

"We need to follow the instructions exactly," Lisa said, her voice steady despite the fear gnawing at her. "One mistake, and we could make things worse."

Mark's equipment beeped frantically, indicating a surge in paranormal activity. "The readings are off the charts," he said, his voice tight with tension. "We need to be careful."

Sarah closed her eyes, focusing her energy on the ritual. "I can feel their pain," she said softly. "The spirits are desperate for release."

As they began the ritual, the air grew colder, and the oppressive atmosphere became almost unbearable. The malevolent presence seemed to grow stronger, its dark energy pulsating through the walls. The team could feel the weight of the mansion's dark history pressing down on them, but they knew they had to press on.

The ancient symbols and artifacts glowed with an eerie light as they chanted the incantations. The smell of burning herbs filled the air, and the oppressive silence was shattered by the sound of ghostly whispers and the crackling of dark energy.

The malevolent presence seemed to resist, its dark energy pulsating through the walls and attempting to disrupt the ritual. The team could feel the crushing weight pressing down on them, as if the very air was trying to suffocate them.

"We need to stay focused," Alex said, his voice steady despite the fear gnawing at him. "We can't let the spirits stop us."

The team continued the ritual, their determination unwavering. The oppressive atmosphere and the violent paranormal activity left them shaken and scared, but they knew they had to press on.

Finally, with a final agonized scream, the dark energy began to dissipate, and the oppressive atmosphere seemed to lift slightly. The team could feel the malevolent presence retreating.

"We did it," Lisa said, her voice filled with relief. "We completed the ritual."

But the team knew their work was far from over. The oppressive atmosphere and the violent paranormal activity left them shaken and scared, but they knew they had to uncover the truth about Black Hollow and put the spirits to rest, no matter the cost.

19

BREAKING THE CURSE

The oppressive atmosphere seemed to lift slightly, but the team knew their ordeal was far from over. They had completed the ritual and weakened the mansion's power, but the malevolent presence still lingered. They needed to break the curse once and for all to put the spirits to rest.

The team gathered their courage and made their way to the heart of the mansion. The walls pulsed with a dark, sinister energy, and the air was thick with tension. The smell of decay and old blood filled their nostrils, making it hard to breathe.

"We need to find the core of this place," Lisa said, her voice steady despite the fear gnawing at her. "That's where we'll find the source of its power."

Mark's equipment beeped frantically, indicating a surge in paranormal activity. "The readings are off the charts," he said, his voice tight with tension. "We're getting close."

As they moved through the darkened halls, the oppressive atmosphere grew heavier. The sense of dread became almost unbearable, and the temperature continued to drop. The team could feel the malevolent presence watching them, its gaze heavy and malevolent.

They reached a large, ornate door, its surface covered in intricate carvings of ancient symbols. The air around it crackled with dark energy, and the oppressive atmosphere became suffocating.

"This is it," Alex said, his voice filled with determination. "This is the heart of the mansion."

The team exchanged worried glances, but they knew they had to press on. They pushed open the heavy door, revealing a large chamber filled with dark, pulsating veins. The air was thick with the smell of decay and old blood, and the temperature had dropped to freezing.

The oppressive atmosphere and the sense of being watched never left them, making every moment feel like a prelude to something terrible. The malevolent presence seemed to grow stronger, its dark energy pulsating through the walls.

"We need to destroy this place," Lisa said, her voice trembling. "It's the only way to break the curse."

The team moved cautiously through the chamber, their flashlights casting eerie shadows on the walls. The air grew colder, and the oppressive atmosphere became almost unbearable.

Suddenly, the room was plunged into darkness, and the oppressive silence was shattered by the sound of ghostly whispers and the smell of burning herbs. The team felt a crushing weight pressing down on them, as if the very air was trying to suffocate them.

The malevolent presence seemed to grow stronger, its dark energy pulsating through the walls. The team could feel the weight of the mansion's dark history pressing down on them, but they knew they had to press on.

"We need to destroy these symbols," Alex said, his voice steady despite the fear gnawing at him. "It's the only way to break the curse."

Sarah focused her energy, trying to connect with the spirits and push the malevolent force away. The air grew colder, and the smell of decay intensified. The sense of dread became almost unbearable.

As they began to destroy the symbols, the walls around them seemed to come alive, twisting and writhing as if in agony. The oppressive atmosphere and the violent paranormal activity left them shaken and scared, but they knew they had to press on.

Finally, with a final agonized scream, the dark energy began to dissipate, and the oppressive atmosphere seemed to lift slightly. The team could feel the malevolent presence retreating.

"We did it," Lisa said, her voice filled with relief. "We weakened the mansion's power."

But the team knew their work was far from over. The oppressive atmosphere and the violent paranormal activity left them shaken and scared, but they knew they had to uncover the truth about Black Hollow and put the spirits to rest, no matter the cost.

20

THE GHOSTLY HORDE

The oppressive atmosphere seemed to lift slightly, but the team knew their ordeal was far from over. They had weakened the mansion's power, but the malevolent presence still lingered. They needed to face the final confrontation to break the curse and put the spirits to rest once and for all.

The team gathered their courage and prepared for the final confrontation. They knew it would be dangerous, but they were determined to put an end to the mansion's dark history and free the trapped spirits.

Lisa gathered the ancient texts and artifacts they had discovered, carefully laying them out in the center of the chamber. The air was thick with tension, and the temperature continued to drop. The oppressive atmosphere and the sense of being watched never left them, making every moment feel like a prelude to something terrible.

"We need to stay focused," Alex said, his voice steady despite the fear gnawing at him. "This is our last chance to break the curse."

Mark's equipment beeped frantically, indicating a surge in paranormal activity. "The readings are off the charts," he said, his voice tight with tension. "We need to be careful."

Sarah closed her eyes, focusing her energy on the ritual. "I can feel their pain," she said softly. "The spirits are desperate for release."

As they began the final ritual, the air grew colder, and the oppressive atmosphere became almost unbearable. The malevolent presence seemed to grow stronger, its dark energy pulsating through the walls. The team could feel the weight of the mansion's dark history pressing down on them, but they knew they had to press on.

The ancient symbols and artifacts glowed with an eerie light as they chanted the incantations. The smell of burning herbs filled the air, and the oppressive silence was shattered by the sound of ghostly whispers and the crackling of dark energy.

Suddenly, the room was filled with the ghostly apparitions of the mansion's former inhabitants. The spirits moved with an eerie grace, their faces twisted in sorrow and despair. The team could feel the weight of their suffering pressing down on them.

"We need to finish the ritual," Alex said, his voice steady despite the fear gnawing at him. "It's the only way to put them to rest."

The team continued the ritual, their determination unwavering. The oppressive atmosphere and the violent paranormal activity left them shaken and scared, but they knew they had to press on.

The ghostly apparitions seemed to grow more agitated, their whispers turning into screams. The air crackled with dark energy, and the oppressive atmosphere became almost unbearable. But the team pressed on, their determination unwavering.

Finally, with a final agonized scream, the dark energy began to dissipate, and the oppressive atmosphere seemed to lift slightly. The team could feel the malevolent presence retreating, and the ghostly apparitions began to fade.

"We did it," Lisa said, her voice filled with relief. "We broke the curse."

The oppressive atmosphere and the violent

paranormal activity left them shaken and scared, but the team knew they had finally put an end to the mansion's dark history. The spirits were free, and the curse was broken.

21

THE ESCAPE

The oppressive atmosphere seemed to lift completely as the curse was broken. The team felt a sense of relief wash over them, knowing that they had put an end to the mansion's dark history and freed the trapped spirits.

As they gathered their equipment and prepared to leave, the mansion seemed to come alive with a new energy. The walls no longer pulsed with dark energy, and the air was no longer thick with tension. The oppressive silence had given way to a peaceful stillness.

"We did it," Alex said, his voice filled with relief. "We finally put an end to the curse."

The team made their way to the grand entrance, the heavy wooden doors creaking open as if welcoming them to their freedom. The air outside was fresh and cool, a stark contrast to the oppressive atmosphere inside the mansion.

As they stepped out into the sunlight, they felt a sense of accomplishment and relief. The mansion stood silent behind them; its dark history finally laid to rest.

"We should document everything," Lisa said, her voice steady. "The world needs to know what happened here."

Mark nodded, his equipment still beeping softly. "We've got plenty of evidence," he said, his voice filled with satisfaction. "This will be one for the history books."

Sarah looked back at the mansion, her eyes filled with a mixture of sorrow and relief. "The spirits are finally at peace," she said softly. "Their suffering is over."

The team knew that their journey was far from over. There were still other mysteries to uncover and other spirits to help. But for now, they could take solace in knowing that they had made a difference.

As they drove away from Black Hollow, the mansion stood silent and still, a testament to the power of determination and courage. The team knew that they would carry the memory of their ordeal with them, but they were also filled with a sense of hope and purpose.

They had faced their fears and emerged victorious, and they knew that they could face whatever challenges lay ahead. The world was full of mysteries, and they were ready to uncover them, one haunted mansion at a time.

EPILOGUE: THE RETURN

Years later, the story of Black Hollow became a legend in paranormal circles. The mansion stood as a silent monument to the bravery of the team who had freed the trapped spirits and broken the curse.

Alex, Lisa, Mark, and Sarah continued their work as paranormal investigators, their bond strengthened by their shared ordeal. They traveled the world, uncovering the secrets of haunted places and helping spirits find peace.

But Black Hollow always held a special place in their hearts. It was the place where they had faced their greatest challenge and emerged victorious. It was the place where they had learned the true power of determination and courage.

And so, every year, they returned to Black Hollow to pay their respects to the spirits they had freed and to remind themselves of the importance of their work. The mansion stood silent and still, a testament to the power of their bravery and determination.

As they stood before the grand entrance, the sun setting behind them, they knew that they would continue their work, no matter the cost. They were paranormal investigators, and they were ready to face whatever challenges lay ahead.

The world was full of mysteries, and they were determined to uncover them, one haunted mansion at a time. And they knew that, no matter what, they would always have each other.

The End.

ABOUT THE AUTHOR

Zarua D. Maning is an author known for weaving intricate tales of suspense, mystery, and the supernatural. With a passion for exploring the unknown and a talent for creating vivid, immersive worlds, Zarua's books have captivated readers around the globe.

Growing up with a deep curiosity for the paranormal, Zarua spent countless nights reading ghost stories and legends, which fueled an imagination that knows no bounds. This fascination with the supernatural led to a career in writing that seamlessly blends spine-tingling horror with profound emotional depth.

Zarua's storytelling is marked by a unique ability to delve into the human psyche, exploring themes of fear, redemption, and the enduring power of the human spirit. Each book is a journey into the heart of darkness, where characters confront their deepest fears and discover the strength within.

When not writing, Zarua is an avid traveler, seeking inspiration from the world's most mysterious and haunting locations. An animal lover and advocate for the voiceless, Zarua dedicates time to causes that make the world a better place.

Living a life filled with passion for art, love, and the unexplained, Zarua is grateful for the support of readers, friends, and family who have been part of this incredible journey. With every book, Zarua strives to give a voice to those who have been silenced and to create stories that resonate deeply with the soul.

ACKNOWLEDGMENTS

To my readers—

Your unwavering support and enthusiasm have been the driving force behind every word written and every story told. Your love for these tales fuels my passion and pushes me to explore the deepest corners of my imagination. Thank you for embarking on these journeys with me, for your kind words, and for believing in the magic and mystery of my stories. Without you, none of this would be possible.

To my family—

Your love and support are the foundation upon which all my dreams are built. You have been my rock, my inspiration, and my sanctuary. In every late night and early morning, in every moment of doubt and triumph, you have stood by my side, encouraging me to pursue my passion with unwavering faith.

To my parents, who nurtured my love for reading and storytelling from a young age. Your endless encouragement and belief in me have been a beacon of light in the darkest of times. I miss you everyday.

To my siblings, who have been my first audience and my biggest cheerleaders. Your laughter, your feedback, and your constant support have been invaluable.

To my wonderful husband, who has been my anchor in this journey. Your love, patience, and understanding have given me the strength to keep going, even when the path seemed uncertain.

And to all the extended family and friends who have been there through thick and thin, thank you for your love and for always being there.

To God—

Thank You for the gift of creativity and for guiding me through every challenge. Your grace and blessings have been my constant companion, providing me with the strength and inspiration to persevere. I am forever grateful for Your love and guidance in every step of this journey.

The power of family is the heartbeat of my stories, and your presence in my life is the greatest gift I could ever ask for. This book, and every book, is a testament to the love, strength, and unwavering support you have given me.

With all my heart,

Zarua D. Maning